Only Eight

By Julia Thomas and Kristi Thomas-Soares

RESOURCE *Publications* • Eugene, Oregon

Resource Publications
A division of Wipf and Stock Publishers
199 W 8th Ave, Suite 3
Eugene, OR 97401

Only Eight
By Thomas, Julia and Thomas-Soares, Kristi
Copyright©2016 by Thomas, Julia
ISBN 13: 978-1-5326-9663-3
Publication date 2/11/2020
Previously published by Green Ivy Publishing, 2016

I know I'm only eight years old, but I can make a difference. I may not be able to drive or vote or even walk to the store by myself, but I know I can make a difference.

It all started on the first day of third grade when my teacher, Mrs. Stanford, asked each of us to write a goal for this school year. Gabriel wanted to get A's on his tests. Nora wanted to score at least one goal in soccer. Ava wanted to stop fighting with her sister. I didn't know what my goal should be. That day at lunch, while eating my turkey sandwich, it came to me: I was going to make a difference and help others! With my goal firmly taped to my desk so I could remember what I wanted to do, it was time to put my plan into action.

In September, as the leaves were changing colors, I took care of my neighbor's two big dogs. I was glad that I could help them enjoy their vacation.

In October, when it was windy, I helped pick up the trash at my school that the wind had blown all over our campus. I was happy to see our school clean again.

In November, the month when we give thanks, I volunteered at a food bank. I helped pass out food to families who needed a little help that month. I was thankful that I could help another family enjoy a meal.

In December, as the days became shorter, I decided to visit a nearby retirement home and play some festive songs on the piano. I was excited to see all the smiles as I played the familiar tunes.

In January, when it was wet and rainy, I helped my family make sack lunches to pass out to the homeless in our community. I felt brave for helping these people that I had always been a little scared of.

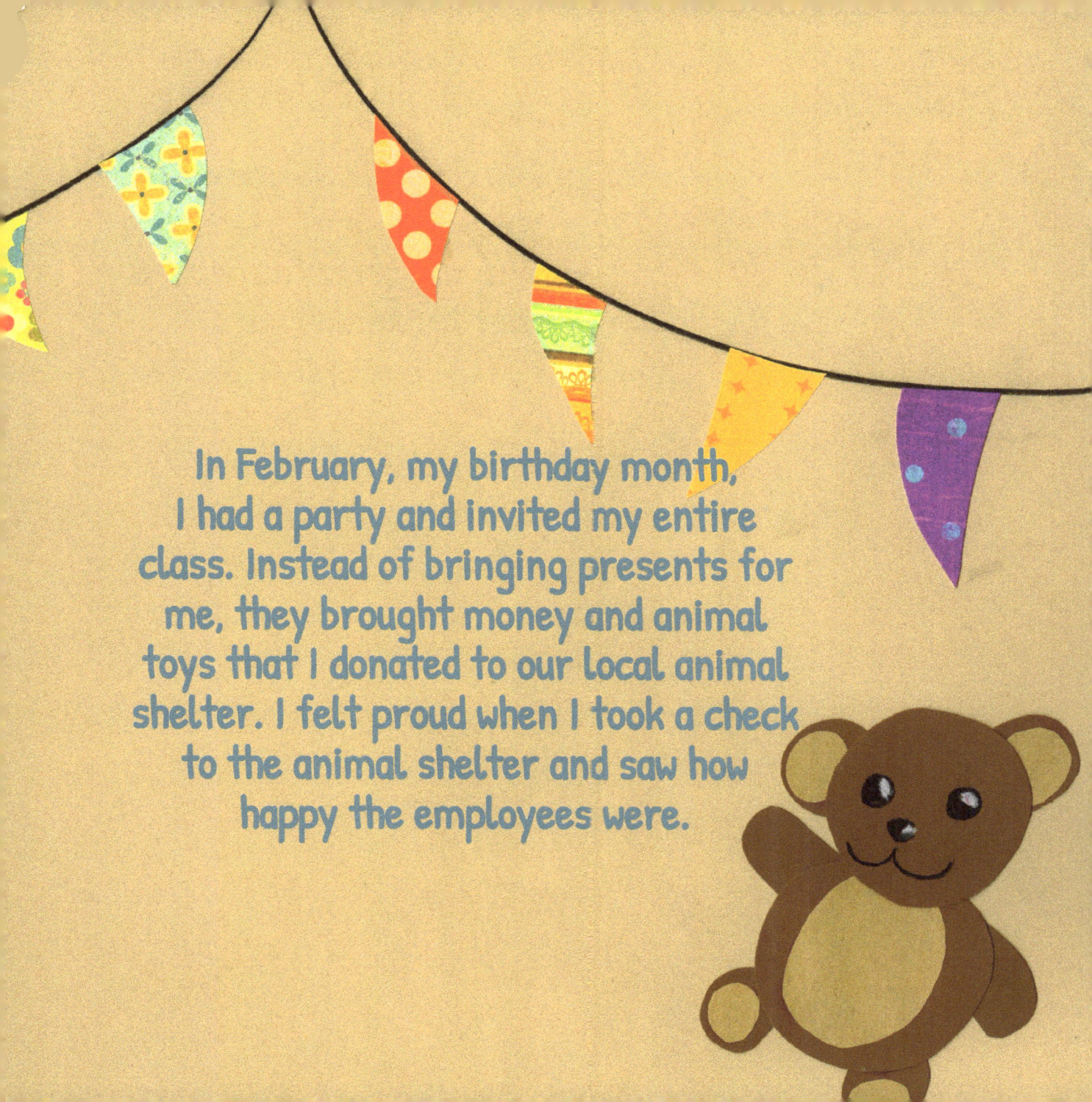

In February, my birthday month, I had a party and invited my entire class. Instead of bringing presents for me, they brought money and animal toys that I donated to our local animal shelter. I felt proud when I took a check to the animal shelter and saw how happy the employees were.

In March, when I was ready for spring, I spent a weekend helping my grandma around her house and yard.

I felt grown-up knowing that I helped my grandma do things she couldn't do by herself.

In April, when the days were long and sunny, I had a lemonade stand and was busy with lots of customers. I felt thrilled when I realized that the money I earned would buy hot meals for 34 people at our local homeless shelter.

In May, during our spring cleaning, I helped clean out all of our closets. We took a truck full of clothes and toys to donate to a thrift store. The money will help veterans and their families.

I felt productive knowing our house was clean and we were helping other people.

In June, when school was letting out for the summer, I spent a Saturday at the beach picking up trash that others had left behind. I felt relaxed when I looked around and saw a clean beach.

Even though I was only eight years old, I know I made a difference last year. Imagine what I'll be able to do this year now that I'm nine!

www.ingramcontent.com/pod-product-compliance
Lightning Source LLC
Chambersburg PA
CBHW041134170626
46815CB00009B/359